Laura's Pa

THE COMPLETE
LAURA CHAPTER BOOK COLLECTION

Adapted from the Little House books
by Laura Ingalls Wilder
Illustrated by Renée Graef and Doris Ettlinger

LITTLE HOUSE

Laura #12

Laura's Pa

ADAPTED FROM THE LITTLE HOUSE BOOKS BY

Laura Ingalls Wilder

ILLUSTRATED BY

Renée Graef

HarperTrophy®
A Division of HarperCollinsPublishers

Adaptation by Heather Henson.

Illustrations for this book are inspired by the work of Garth Williams with his permission, which we gratefully acknowledge.

HarperCollins®, ✦®, Little House®, Harper Trophy®, and The Laura Years™ are trademarks of HarperCollins Publishers Inc.

Library of Congress Cataloging-in-Publication Data
Laura's pa : [adapted from the text by] Laura Ingalls Wilder /
  illustrated by Renée Graef.
    p.   cm. — (A Little House chapter book)
  Summary: Stories about Laura's father and life on the frontier.
  ISBN 0-06-027896-X (lib. bdg.). — ISBN 0-06-442082-5 (pbk.)
  1. Wilder, Laura Ingalls, 1867–1957—Juvenile fiction. [1. Wilder, Laura
Ingalls, 1867–1957—Fiction. 2. Wilder, Almanzo—Fiction. 3. Frontier
and pioneer life—Fiction. 4. Family life—Fiction. 5. Fathers—Fiction.]
I. Wilder, Laura Ingalls, 1867–1957. II. Graef, Renée, ill.
PZ7.L37274 1999   98-20344
[Fic]—dc21   CIP
                                                                          AC

❖
First Harper Trophy edition, 1999

Contents

CHAPTER 1

Little House in the Big Woods

Laura lived in the Big Woods of Wisconsin in a little gray house made of logs. The great, dark trees of the Big Woods stood all around the house. There were no other houses nearby. There were no roads. There were no people. There were only trees and the wild animals who made the Big Woods their home.

At night, Laura lay awake in the little trundle bed she shared with her sister

Mary, and she listened in the dark. She could not hear anything at all but the sound of the trees whispering together. Sometimes, far away in the night, a wolf howled.

It was a scary sound. Laura knew that wolves could eat little girls. But she also knew that her Pa would never let anything happen to her. Pa's arms were strong, and his eyes sparkled blue when he smiled. He had built the log house from good solid logs. He kept his gun over the door, and he always kept watch over Ma and Laura and Mary and their baby sister, Carrie.

Still, Laura's eyes would open wide when she heard the howling of the wolf moving closer in the night.

"Go to sleep, Laura," Pa would gently say. "Jack won't let the wolves in."

Jack was their good old bulldog. He lay

on the floor in front of the door, keeping watch, too.

So Laura would snuggle deeper under the covers of the trundle bed, close beside Mary, and go to sleep.

One night, Laura heard two wolves howling. Pa saw that Laura could not go to sleep. He picked her up out of bed and carried her over to the window so that she could see the wolves.

The two wolves were sitting right in front of the house. They looked like big, shaggy dogs. They pointed their sharp noses at the bright moon and howled.

Jack paced up and down in front of the door, growling. The hair on his back stood up, and he showed his sharp, fierce teeth.

The wolves howled, but they could not get in. Laura felt safe and warm with Pa beside her.

In the morning, the wolves were gone. Pa went out to do his chores around the farm. Pa worked hard all day long. Ma worked hard too, doing all the work that had to be done around the house. Laura and Mary helped. After the day's work was done, Ma sometimes cut paper dolls for Laura and Mary to play with.

But the best time of all was at night,

4

right before supper, when Pa came home.

In the winter, Pa would come into the warm house after tramping through the snowy woods. He would have tiny icicles hanging on the ends of his mustache. He would hang his gun on the wall over the door. Then he would throw off his fur cap and coat and mittens, and call, "Where's my little half-pint of sweet cider half drunk up?"

That was Laura, because she was so small.

Laura and Mary would run to climb on his knees. They would sit on his lap while he warmed himself by the fire.

After he was all warmed up, he would play a game with Laura and Mary. One game they loved was called mad dog.

Pa would run his fingers through his thick, brown hair, standing it all up on end.

He would drop down on all fours and start growling. Then he would chase Laura and Mary all around the room. He would try to get them cornered where they couldn't get away.

Laura and Mary were quick at dodging and running, and Pa usually couldn't catch them. But one night he did catch them against the wood box, behind the stove. They couldn't get past Pa, and there was no other way out.

Pa let out a terrible growl. His hair was wild and his eyes were fierce. Suddenly, it all seemed real. Mary was so frightened that she could not move. Laura looked at Pa and thought about the wolves in the night. As Pa came nearer, she screamed. With a wild leap and a scramble, she went over the wood box, dragging Mary with her.

All at once, there was no mad dog at

all. There was only Pa standing there with his blue eyes shining, looking at Laura.

"Well!" he said to her. "You're only a little half-pint of cider half drunk up, but by Jinks! You're as strong as a little French horse!"

"You shouldn't frighten the children so, Charles," Ma said softly. "Look how big their eyes are."

Pa looked, and then he took down his fiddle. He began to play and sing so they wouldn't be frightened anymore.

> *"Yankee Doodle went to town,*
> *He wore his striped trousies,*
> *He swore he couldn't see the town,*
> *There was so many houses."*

Laura and Mary forgot all about the mad dog. Pa kept time with his foot. Laura and Mary clapped their hands to the music while he sang.

> *"And I'll sing Yankee Doodle-de-do,*
> *And I'll sing Yankee Doodle,*
> *And I'll sing Yankee Doodle-de-do,*
> *And I'll sing Yankee Doodle!"*

All alone in the Big Woods, the little log house was cozy and warm. The fire was shining on the hearth, and Jack lay blinking at the jumping flames. Everything was merry and bright when Pa played his fiddle and sang in his deep, happy voice.

CHAPTER 2

Pa Tells a Story

At night, after the supper dishes had been wiped and put away, Laura and Mary would beg Pa to tell them a story. Pa would take them on his knees and tickle their faces with his long whiskers until they laughed.

"Tell us about the Voice in the Woods," Laura begged him one night. She had heard the story many times before, but she always loved hearing it again.

Pa's blue eyes twinkled. "Oh, no!" he said. "You don't want to hear about the time I was a naughty little boy."

9

"Oh, yes, we do! We do!" Laura and Mary cried together.

So Pa began the story.

"When I was a little boy, **not** much bigger than Mary, I had to go every afternoon to find the cows in the woods and drive them home. My father told me never to stop and play. He said I must hurry to bring the cows home before dark, because there were bears and wolves and panthers in the woods."

Laura shuddered. She had never seen a panther, but Pa had told her stories about them.

"One day," Pa continued, "I started earlier than usual, so I thought I did not need to hurry. There were so many things to see in the woods. Soon I forgot that dark was coming. There were red squirrels in the trees, chipmunks running through

10

the leaves, and little rabbits playing games together in the open places. Little rabbits always play games together before bed, you know."

Laura smiled to think of little rabbits playing games.

"I began to pretend I was a mighty hunter, stalking the wild animals, until the woods seemed full of wild creatures," Pa said. "And then, all at once, I heard the birds twittering 'good night.' I looked around and saw that the path was full of shadows. The woods were dark.

"I knew that I must get the cows home quickly, or it would be black night before they were safe in the barn. But I couldn't find the cows!

"I listened, but I could not hear their bells. I called, but the cows didn't come.

"I was afraid of the dark and the wild

11

beasts, but I dared not go home to my father without the cows. So I ran through the woods, hunting and calling. All the time the shadows were getting thicker and darker. The woods seemed larger. The trees and the bushes looked strange.

"I could not find the cows anywhere. I climbed up hills, looking and calling. I went down into dark hollows, calling and looking. I stopped and listened for the cowbells. There was not a sound but the rustling of leaves.

"Then I heard loud breathing and thought a panther was there, in the dark behind me. But it was only my own breathing.

"My bare legs were scratched by the briers. When I ran through the bushes, their branches struck me. But I kept on looking and calling.

"'Sukey! Sukey!' I shouted with all my might. 'Sukey!'

"Right over my head something asked, 'Who?'

"My hair stood on end.

"'Who? Who?' the Voice said again. And then *how* I ran!

"I forgot all about the cows. All I wanted was to get out of the dark woods, to get home.

"That thing in the dark came after me and called again, 'Who-oo?'

"I ran with all my might. I ran till I couldn't breathe, and still I kept on running. Something grabbed my foot, and I went down. But I jumped up right away and kept running. Not even a wolf could have caught me.

"At last I came out of the dark woods, by the barn. There stood all the cows,

waiting to be let through the bars. I let them in and then ran to the house.

"My father looked up and said, 'Young man, what makes you so late? Did you stop and play?'"

Pa stopped telling the story and waited, smiling down at Laura and Mary.

"Go on, Pa!" Laura cried. "Please go on."

"Well," said Pa, "then your grandpa gave me a good spanking, so that I would remember to mind him after that.

"'A big boy nine years old is old enough to remember to mind,' he said. 'There's a good reason for what I tell you to do,' he said, 'and if you'll do as you're told, no harm will come to you.'"

"Yes, yes, Pa!" Laura said, bouncing up and down on Pa's knee. "And then what did he say?"

"He said, 'If you'd obeyed me, you wouldn't have been out in the Big Woods after dark, and you wouldn't have been scared by a screech owl.'"

Laura laughed and laughed, and so did Mary. It was funny to think of Pa being scared by an old screech owl.

CHAPTER 3

A New House

When spring came to the Big Woods, Laura and Mary helped Ma and Pa pack all their belongings in a covered wagon. They were moving west to the Kansas prairie.

For weeks and weeks, the covered wagon rolled through woods and over rivers, until finally it came to the great empty prairie.

There were hardly any trees on the prairie. There was only tall, wild grass as far as Laura could see. Overhead, the big blue sky seemed to go on forever.

17

One day, Pa stopped the wagon in the middle of all that emptiness.

"Here we are, Caroline!" he said to Ma. "We'll build our house right here."

Laura and Mary scrambled down from the wagon. All around, the tall grass blew in the warm, gentle breeze. Rabbits and prairie chickens darted in between the stalks. Grasshoppers buzzed, and meadowlarks went springing straight up into the clear, blue sky.

To the north, Laura and Mary could just see a line of green treetops. That was a creek bed, Pa told them. On the prairie, trees could only grow near a river or a creek.

To the east, they saw another line of green.

"That's the Verdigris River," Pa said, pointing it out to Ma.

Right away, Pa and Ma began to

 18

unload the wagon. They took everything out and piled it on the ground. Pa took off the wagon cover and put it over the pile, while Laura and Mary and Jack watched.

Then Pa got into the wagon. He drove right down into the prairie, out of sight.

"Where's Pa going?" Laura asked.

"He's going to get a load of logs from the creek bottoms," Ma answered.

For days, Pa hauled load after load of logs. He put the logs into two piles. One pile was for a house, and one was for a stable.

When Pa had enough logs, he began to build the house.

First, he paced off the size of the house on the ground. Then he took his spade and dug two little hollows. Into the hollows he rolled two of the biggest logs. He made sure they were sound, strong

19

logs because they would hold up the house. Pa said they were called sills.

Next, Pa took his ax and cut a wide, deep notch into each end of the sills. He took two more strong logs and cut notches into their ends. When the notches were cut, he rolled each log over so that the notches fit down over the notches in the sills.

Now there was an empty square on the ground, one log high. That was the foundation of the house.

The next day, Pa began to build up the walls. He notched each log before carefully rolling it up and fitting it snugly over the log below it. There were cracks in between the logs, but that did not matter, because Pa would chink those cracks.

Every day, the walls were a little higher. Soon, Laura couldn't climb over them anymore.

One afternoon, Pa stopped working on the house and drove off in the wagon. He was going hunting so they would have something good to eat for supper. When he came back that evening, he was whistling.

"Good news!" he shouted when he saw them.

They had a neighbor. Pa had met him in the woods. His name was Mr. Edwards, and he lived alone on the other side of the creek. Pa and Mr. Edwards were going to trade work, and that would make building the house easier.

"He's going to help me finish our house," Pa said. "Then as soon as he gets his logs ready, I'll go over and help him."

"That's good, Charles," Ma said. "I'm glad."

Early the next morning, Mr. Edwards

came. He was lean and tall and brown. He bowed to Ma and called her "Ma'am," politely. But he told Laura that he was a wildcat from Tennessee.

He wore tall boots and a ragged sweater. On his head he wore a coonskin cap. He could spit tobacco juice farther than Laura had ever imagined anyone could spit tobacco juice. He could hit anything he spit at, too.

Laura tried and tried, but she could never spit so far or so well as Mr. Edwards could.

Mr. Edwards was a fast worker. In one day he and Pa built the walls as high as Pa wanted them. They joked and sang while they worked, and their axes made the chips fly.

On top of the walls they set up a skeleton roof of thin poles. The poles were called rafters. Then they cut a tall hole into one of the walls for a door, and they cut two square windows.

As soon as the holes were cut, Laura ran inside. Stripes of sunshine came through the cracks in the wall. The stripes of sunshine were all across Laura's hands and her arms and her bare feet. Laura could see stripes of prairie through the cracks. The sweet smell of grass mixed with the sweet smell of cut wood.

Now the house was finished, all but the roof. Pa would build the roof by himself. In the meantime, they would drape the wagon cover over the rafters.

The walls were solid, and the house was large. Laura couldn't wait to sleep inside it.

Mr. Edwards said he would go home

now, but Pa and Ma said he must stay to supper. Ma cooked an especially good supper because they had company.

There was stewed jackrabbit with white-flour dumplings and plenty of gravy. There was a steaming-hot, thick corn bread flavored with bacon fat. There was molasses to eat on the corn bread.

Mr. Edwards said he surely did appreciate that supper.

When they were finished eating and the dishes were put away, Pa brought out his fiddle. Mr. Edwards stretched out on the ground to listen.

First, Pa played for Laura and Mary. He played their favorite song, and he sang it. Laura liked the song best of all because on the last line, Pa's voice went down deep, deep, deeper.

 24

"Oh, I am a Gypsy King!
I come and go as I please!
I pull my old nightcap down
And take the world at my ease."

Then his voice went deep, deep down, deeper than the very oldest bullfrog's.

"Oh,
　　　　I am
　　　　　　a
　　　　　　　　Gyp
　　　　　　　　　　sy
　　　　　　　　　　　KING!"

They all laughed. Laura could hardly stop laughing.

"Oh, sing it again, Pa!" Laura cried.

Pa went on playing, and everything began to dance. Mr. Edwards rose up on

25

one elbow. Then he sat up, then he jumped up, and he danced. He danced like a jumping jack in the moonlight. Pa's fiddle kept on rollicking, and his foot kept tapping the ground. Laura's hands and Mary's hands were clapping together, and their feet were patting the ground, too.

"You're the fiddlin'est fool that ever I did see!" Mr. Edwards shouted to Pa. He didn't stop dancing, and Pa didn't stop playing.

Baby Carrie couldn't sleep in all that music. She sat up in Ma's lap, looking at Mr. Edwards with round eyes, clapping her little hands and laughing.

Even the firelight danced, and all along the edges of the fire, the shadows were dancing, too. Only the new house that Pa and Mr. Edwards had built stood still and quiet in the moonlight.

CHAPTER 4

A Strong Door

There were wolves on the prairie, just as there had been in the Big Woods. One night, Laura heard them howling. Then she saw them through the window hole. Even though there was only a quilt covering the doorway, Pa and Jack kept them all safe in the night. But in the morning, right after breakfast, Pa said he would build a strong door for the little log house.

There were no more nails, and the nearest town was forty miles away. But Pa said, "A man doesn't need nails to build a house or make a door."

Pa hitched up the horses, Pet and Patty, to the wagon. He took up his ax and drove off to get more logs to make a door.

Laura helped wash the dishes and make the beds. But when Pa came back, he said she could help him make the door. She could hand him his tools.

With the saw, Pa sawed logs the right length for a door. He sawed shorter logs for the crosspieces. Then with the ax he split the logs into slabs and smoothed them nicely. He laid the long slabs together on the ground and placed the shorter cross-pieces across them. Then he used a tool to make holes through the crosspieces into the long slabs. Into every hole he drove a wooden peg that fit tightly.

Now the door was finished. It was a good oak door, solid and strong.

Next, Pa made hinges to hold the door

in place. He cut three long straps of strong leather for the hinges. One hinge would go at the top of the door, one near the bottom, and one in the middle.

"I told you a fellow doesn't need nails!" Pa said to Laura cheerfully.

When he had fastened the three hinges to the door, he set the door in the doorway. It was a perfect fit. Laura stood against the door to hold it in place while Pa fastened the hinges to the door frame.

Then Pa made a latch on the door so they could open and close it easily. When Pa was finished, Laura pushed the door shut. Pa showed her how to work the latch from the inside. With the door closed, nobody could get in.

But there had to be a way to lift the latch from the outside. So Pa made a latchstring. He cut it from a long strip of leather. He tied one end to the latch. Above the latch he made a small hole through the door. Then he pushed the end of the latchstring through the hole.

Laura stood outside. When the end of the latchstring came through the hole, she took hold of it and pulled. She could pull it hard enough to lift the latch and let herself in.

When the latchstring was out, if you wanted to come in, you pulled the latchstring. But if you were inside and wanted to keep someone out, you pulled the latchstring in through its hole. Then nobody could get in.

It was a good door. Now they wouldn't have to worry about wolves coming into the house.

"I call that a good day's work!" said Pa. "And I had a fine little helper!"

He hugged the top of Laura's head with his hand. Then he gathered up his tools and put them away, whistling as he went.

CHAPTER 5

Building a Chimney

Afew days later, Pa began to build a chimney for Ma so she wouldn't have to cook outdoors anymore.

He chose a place opposite the door. Outside the house, close to the log wall, he cleared away the grass and scraped the ground smooth.

Then he hitched up the horses to the wagon. He was going to the creek to get rocks for the chimney. He whistled as he climbed into the wagon and took the reins.

Then he looked down at Laura, and his eyes sparkled.

"Want to go along, Laura?" he asked. "You and Mary?"

Ma said they could. They quickly climbed up beside Pa on the high wagon seat.

Pet and Patty started with a little jump. The wagon jolted along the wagon trail that Pa had cut into the ground by making so many trips to the creek.

Laura and Mary and Pa rolled across the high prairie, and then down into the creek bottoms. They passed patches of small trees, and Laura saw deer lying in the shadows. The deer lifted their heads and pricked their ears, watching the wagon with soft, large eyes.

All along the wagon trail, there were small flowers blossoming pink and blue and white. Birds balanced on the tops of the tall grasses. Butterflies fluttered in the air.

34

In the lowest part of the creek bed,
the creek was running. Laura couldn't
see the prairie anymore. She could only
see the high dirt walls of the creek.

Pa stopped the wagon beside the
running water.

"You girls can play," he said, "but don't
go out of my sight and don't go into the
water. And don't play with snakes. Some

of the snakes down here are poisonous."

So Laura and Mary played beside the creek while Pa dug rocks and loaded them into the wagon.

Laura and Mary watched the long-legged water bugs skate over the glassy, still pools. They ran along the bank to scare the frogs, and laughed when the green-coated frogs plopped into the water.

There was no wind along the creek. The air was still and warm.

Swarms of mosquitoes buzzed at Laura and Mary. They slapped at mosquitoes on their faces and necks and hands and legs. They looked at the creek and wished they could go wading. They were so hot and itchy, and the water looked so cool.

Laura was sure that it would do no harm just to dip one foot in. When Pa's back was turned, she almost did it.

"Laura," said Pa in a low voice, and she snatched the naughty foot back. "If you girls want to go wading, you can do it in that shallow place. Don't go in over your ankles."

Mary waded only for a little while. She said the small rocks hurt her feet. She sat on a log and patiently slapped at mosquitoes.

The rocks hurt Laura's feet, too, but she kept on wading. When she stood still in the water, tiny minnows nibbled at her toes with their tiny mouths. It was a funny feeling. Laura tried and tried to catch a minnow, but they were too fast.

When the wagon was loaded, Pa called, "Come along, girls!"

They climbed back into the wagon seat and rode away from the creek. Up through the woods and hills they went.

37

Soon they were back on the high prairie, where the winds blew and the grasses seemed to sing and whisper and laugh.

Laura had liked playing in the creek bottoms, but she liked the high prairie the best. The prairie was so wide and sweet and clean.

That afternoon, Laura and Mary watched Pa build the chimney. Ma sat sewing in the shade of the house, and Baby Carrie played on a quilt beside her.

First, Pa mixed clay and water into a beautiful, thick mud. He let Laura stir the mud while he laid a row of rocks around the space he had cleared by the log wall. Then, with a wooden paddle, he spread the mud over the rocks. Into the mud he laid another row of rocks, and plastered them over with more mud.

With rocks and mud, and more rocks

and more mud, Pa slowly built up the walls of the chimney. He made it smaller and smaller as he went.

Soon he had to go to the creek for more rocks. Laura and Mary did not go this time. Mary sat beside Ma and sewed on her nine-patch quilt, but Laura mixed another bucket full of mud for Pa.

By the next afternoon, Pa had built a chimney as high as the house. Pa stood back and looked at it. He ran his fingers through his hair.

"You look like a wild man, Charles," Ma said. "You're standing your hair all on end."

"It stands on end, anyway, Caroline," Pa answered with a laugh. "When I was courting you, it never would lie down, no matter how much I slicked it with bear grease."

Pa threw himself down on the grass and rested for a while. Then he hitched up the wagon and headed off to the woods. When he came back, he had a load of young trees. He cut and notched the tree trunks. Then he laid them along the top of the stone chimney, just as he had built up the walls of the house. As he laid them, he plastered them with mud.

Finally, the chimney was finished.

Next Pa went into the house. With his ax and saw he cut a hole in the wall. Behind that part of the wall was the chimney. When the logs of the wall were cut away, the bottom of the chimney became the fireplace.

The fireplace was large enough for Laura and Mary and Baby Carrie to sit in. Its bottom was the ground that Pa had cleared of grass, and its front was the space where Pa had cut away the logs.

On top of the fireplace, Pa laid a thick oak slab and pegged it firmly. That was the mantelshelf.

When the fireplace was finished, Pa and Ma and Mary and Laura stood and admired it. Only Carrie did not care about it. She just laughed and pointed.

Carefully, Ma built a little fire in the new fireplace. She roasted a prairie chicken for supper. And that evening they ate in the log house.

Inside, the house was pleasant. The good roast chicken was juicy in Laura's mouth. Laura looked at Pa and Ma and Mary and Baby Carrie, and she felt happy. It was nice to be living in a house again.

CHAPTER 6

Finishing the House

One day, Pa took the canvas wagon top off the house. They had been using it as a roof. But now Pa was going to build a real roof to keep out the rain.

For days and days, Pa had been hauling logs from the creek bottoms and splitting them into thin, long slabs. Now he had enough long slabs to make the roof. And he had some nails.

Mr. Edwards had lent Pa the nails. At first, Pa hadn't wanted to take them. He said he didn't like to owe anybody. But Mr. Edwards had insisted.

"That's what I call a good neighbor!" Pa said. He would pay Mr. Edwards back every nail as soon as he could make the long trip to town.

Pa pulled the first slab into place. He laid it across the rafters so that the edges stuck out beyond the wall. Then Pa put some nails in his mouth and took his hammer out of his belt. He began to nail the slab to the rafters.

Carefully, he took the nails one by one from his mouth. With ringing blows of the hammer, he drove them into the slab. Every now and then a nail sprang away from the tough oak and went sailing through the air.

Mary and Laura watched it fall. They searched in the grass until they found it. Sometimes the nail was bent. Then Pa carefully pounded it straight again.

43

He would never waste a nail.

When Pa had nailed down two slabs, he got up on them. He laid and nailed more slabs, all the way up to the top of the rafters. The edge of each slab lapped over the edge of the slab below it.

Then he began again on the other side of the house. Soon he had laid the roof all the way up from that side, too.

Then the roof was done. The house was darker than it had been before, because no light came through the slabs. There was not one single crack that would let rain come in.

"You've done a splendid job, Charles," Ma said. "I'm thankful to have a good roof over my head."

"You shall have furniture, too, as fine as I can make it," Pa replied. "I'll make a bedstead as soon as the floor is laid."

Right away, he began to haul more logs. Day after day he hauled logs. When he had enough logs to make the floor, he began to split them. Laura liked to sit on the woodpile and watch him.

With a mighty blow of his ax, Pa made a crack in one end of the log. Into the crack he slipped an iron wedge. He drove the wedge deeper and deeper into the

45

crack with each swing of his ax. Inch by inch, Pa followed the crack up the tough oak log. With each blow, the wood split a little farther.

He would swing the ax high in the air, then bring it down with a grunt from his chest, *"Ugh!"* The ax struck the iron wedge with a sharp *plung!* The ax always struck exactly where Pa wanted it to.

At last, with a tearing, cracking sound, the whole log split. Its two halves lay on the ground, showing the tree's pale insides. Then Pa wiped the sweat from his forehead. He took a fresh grip on the ax, and he started on another log.

One day, the last log was split, and Pa began to lay the floor. He dragged the logs into the house and laid them one by one, flat side up.

With his spade, he scraped the ground

underneath. Then he fit the round side of the log firmly down into it. With his ax he trimmed the edges so that each log fit against the next, with hardly a crack between them.

Then he took the head of the ax in his hand. With little, careful blows he smoothed the wood. He squinted along each log to see that the surface was straight and true. Finally, he ran his hand over the smoothness and nodded.

"Not a splinter!" he said. "That'll be all right for little bare feet to run over."

When he came to the fireplace, he used shorter logs. He left a space of bare earth in front of the fireplace for a hearth. That way, when sparks or coals popped out of the fire, they would not burn the floor.

One day, the floor was all done. It was

47

smooth and firm and hard. It was made of solid oak. Pa said it would last forever.

"Now we're living like civilized folks again," Ma said.

After that Pa filled the cracks in the walls. He drove thin strips of wood into them, and plastered them well with mud, filling every chink.

"That chinking will keep out the wind, no matter how hard it blows," Ma said.

Pa stopped whistling to smile at her. He slapped the last bit of mud between the logs and smoothed it. Then he set down the bucket.

At last, the house was finished.

"I wish we had glass for windows," Pa said.

"We don't need glass, Charles," said Ma.

"Just the same, if I do well with my hunting and trapping this winter, I'm

 48

going to get some glass in town next spring."

They were all happy that night. The fire on the hearth felt good. Even though it was summer, nights on the prairie were cool. The new floor was golden in the flickering firelight. Outside, the night was large and full of stars.

Pa sat for a long time in the doorway. He played his fiddle and sang to Laura and Mary and Ma inside and to the starry night outside.

CHAPTER 7

Digging a Well

One morning, Pa marked a large circle near the corner of the house. With his spade he cleared away the grass inside the circle. Then he began to shovel out the earth, digging himself deeper and deeper down.

Pa was digging a well so they would have fresh water to drink. He told Laura and Mary that they must never go near the well while he was digging.

From a distance, Laura and Mary watched Pa go deeper and deeper. Even when they couldn't see his head anymore, shovelfuls of earth came flying up.

At last, Laura saw the spade fly up out of the hole. She saw Pa's hands and then his elbows. Then with a heave, Pa came rolling out.

"I can't throw the dirt out any deeper," he said.

He would have to have help now. He took his gun and rode away on Patty. When he came back, he had someone to help with the well. He was going to trade work with their other neighbor, Mr. Scott. Mr. Scott would come help Pa dig the well, and then Pa would help dig Mr. Scott's well.

Ma and Laura and Mary had not seen Mr. and Mrs. Scott. Their house was hidden somewhere in a little valley on the prairie.

At sunup the next morning, Mr. Scott

51

came. He was short and stout. His hair was bleached by the sun, and his skin was bright red.

Laura liked him. Every morning, as soon as the dishes were washed and the beds made, she ran out to watch Mr. Scott and Pa working at the well.

Pa and Mr. Scott had built a machine called a windlass out of strong logs. The windlass stood over the well. It had a handle that turned one of the logs. And it had two buckets attached to a long rope. When the windlass was turned, one bucket went down into the well, and the other bucket came up.

In the morning, Mr. Scott slid down the rope and dug inside the well. He filled the buckets with earth, and Pa hauled them up and emptied them.

In the afternoon, Pa slid down the rope

into the well, and Mr. Scott hauled up the buckets.

Every morning, before Pa would let Mr. Scott go down the rope, he set a candle in a bucket. He lit the candle and lowered it to the bottom.

Once, Pa let Laura peep over the edge. She saw the candle brightly burning, far down in the dark hole in the ground.

Pa would watch the burning candle. Then he would say, "Seems to be all right," and he would pull up the bucket and blow out the candle.

"That's all foolishness, Ingalls," Mr. Scott said. "The well was all right yesterday."

"You can't ever tell," Pa replied. "Better be safe than sorry."

Laura did not know what danger Pa was looking for by that candlelight. She did not ask, because Pa and Mr. Scott were busy.

One morning, Mr. Scott came while Pa was still eating breakfast. They heard him shout, "Hi, Ingalls. It's sunup. Let's go!"

Pa drank his coffee and went out. The windlass began to creak, and Pa began to whistle.

54

Laura and Mary were washing the dishes, and Ma was making the big bed, when Pa's whistling stopped.

"Scott!" Pa shouted. "Scott! Scott!" Then Pa called, "Caroline, come quick."

Ma ran out of the house. Laura ran after her.

"Scott's fainted down there," Pa said. "I've got to go down after him."

"Did you send down the candle?" Ma asked.

"No. I thought he had. I asked him if it was all right, and he said it was." Pa cut the empty bucket off the rope and tied the rope firmly to the windlass.

"Charles, you can't. You mustn't," Ma cried.

"I'll make it all right," Pa said. "I won't breathe till I get out. We can't leave him down there."

"Get on Patty and go for help," Ma pleaded.

"There isn't time," Pa answered.

"Charles, if I can't pull you up—if you keel over down there and I can't pull you up—"

"Caroline, I've got to," Pa said. He swung into the well. His head slid out of sight, down the rope.

Ma crouched and shaded her eyes, staring down into the well.

All over the prairie, meadowlarks were singing. The wind was blowing warmer, but Laura was cold.

Suddenly, Ma jumped up and seized the handle of the windlass. She tugged at it with all her might. The rope strained and the windlass creaked. Laura wanted to help, but Ma had told her to keep back.

Ma pulled and pulled, but the windlass

wouldn't turn. Laura thought that Pa had keeled over down in the well, and Ma couldn't pull him up. But then the wind-lass turned a little, and then a little more.

Suddenly, Pa's hand came up, holding the rope. Then his head came up. His arm held on to the windlass. He pulled himself onto the ground and sat there.

The windlass whirled around and there was a thud deep down in the well. Pa struggled to get up, and Ma said: "Sit still, Charles! Laura, get some water. Quick!"

Laura ran. She came hurrying back, lugging the pail of water. Pa and Ma were both turning the windlass. The rope slowly wound itself up, and the bucket came up out of the well.

Tied to the bucket was Mr. Scott. His arms and his legs and his head hung and wobbled. His mouth was partly open, and his eyes were half shut.

Pa tugged him onto the grass and rolled him over. Then he felt his wrist and listened to his chest.

"He's breathing," Pa said, lying down beside him on the grass. "He'll be all right in the air. I'm all right, Caroline. I'm plumb tuckered out, is all."

Pa explained to Laura and Mary what had happened.

Mr. Scott had breathed a kind of gas that stayed deep in the ground. It stayed at the bottom of wells because it was heavier than air. It could not be seen or smelled. But if you sent a lit candle down into the well, it would go out if the gas was there.

The gas was very dangerous. No one could breathe it very long and live. Pa had gone down into that gas and saved Mr. Scott's life.

"You were right about that candle business, Ingalls," Mr. Scott said when he could speak again. "I thought it was all foolishness and I would not bother with it, but I've found out my mistake."

"Well," said Pa, "where a light can't live, I know I can't. I like to be safe when I can be. But all's well that ends well."

After Mr. Scott went home, Pa lay down for a while. He had breathed a little of the gas, and he needed to rest.

But that afternoon, Pa got up and took a piece of string and a little gunpowder. He tied the powder in a piece of cloth and then tied the cloth to one end of the string.

"Come along, Laura," he said. "I'll show you something."

They went to the well. Pa lit the end of the string and waited till the spark was crawling quickly along it. Then he

59

dropped the little bundle into the well.

In a minute they heard a muffled *bang!* A puff of smoke came out of the well.

"That will bring the gas out of the well," Pa said.

When the smoke was all gone, Pa let Laura light the candle. She stood beside him while he sent it down. All the way down in the dark hole, the little candle kept on burning like a star. That meant the well was safe again.

The next day, Pa and Mr. Scott went on digging the well. But they always sent the candle down every morning and every afternoon.

One day, when Pa was in the well digging, a loud shout came echoing up. Ma and Laura and Mary ran outside.

"Pull, Scott! Pull!" Pa yelled from inside the well.

A swishing, gurgling sound echoed down below. Mr. Scott turned the windlass as fast as he could, and Pa scrambled out of the well, muddy and dripping.

The well was finally filling with water. In no time at all, it was almost full.

Laura looked down into the well, and she saw a little girl's head looking up at her. She waved her hand, and the girl's hand waved, too.

Pa built a wooden platform over the well. There was a hole for the water bucket to go through, and a heavy cover to go over the hole when they weren't using it.

The well water was clear and cold and good. Whenever Laura or Mary was thirsty, Ma lifted the cover and drew a dripping bucket of cold, fresh water from the well that Pa had dug.

CHAPTER 8

Pa Goes to Town

Soon summer was over. The days and nights on the prairie began to get colder. Pa said it was time for him to go to town for supplies. He had not been able to go while it was hot because the heat was too hard on the horses.

Pet and Patty would have to pull the wagon very fast to get to town in two days. Pa did not want to be away from home any longer than he had to.

One morning, before it was light out, Pa went away. When Laura and Mary woke up, he was gone. Everything was

empty and lonely. It was no_____
had only gone hunting. He had g___
town, and he would not be back for fou_
long days.

Laura and Mary helped Ma with the
chores. The good bulldog Jack kept watch
over everything. Jack even growled at Mr.
Edwards when he came to check on them.

The second day Pa was gone was just
as empty as the first. Jack paced around
the stable and around the house. He
would not pay any attention to Laura. He
was uneasy and watchful with Pa gone.

That night, while they sat by the warm
fire, they thought of Pa. If nothing had
delayed him, he would be in town now.
Tomorrow he would be in the store, buy-
ing the things they needed. Then, if he
could get an early start, he could come
partway home and camp on the prairie

... the next night he ...

... the wind was blowing ... cold, Ma kept the door of the little house shut. Laura and Mary ... the fire and listened to the wind as it ... screaming around the house.

In the afternoon, they wondered if Pa was leaving town and coming toward them, against the wind.

Then, when it was dark, they wondered where he was camping. The wind was bitterly cold. It even came into the snug little house. It made their backs shiver while their faces roasted in the heat of the fire. Somewhere on the big, dark, lonesome prairie, Pa was camping in that wind.

The next day was very long. Laura and Mary knew they could not expect Pa in the morning. But they were waiting until they could expect him.

In the afternoon, they began to watch the creek road. Jack was watching it, too.

At choretime, Pa still had not come home. Jack growled at Mr. Edwards when he came to help with the chores. Mr. Edwards told Ma that he could make himself right comfortable with hay in the stable. He would spend the night there if Ma said so.

Ma thanked him nicely, but said she would not put him to that trouble.

"I am expecting Mr. Ingalls any minute now," she told him.

So Mr. Edwards put on his coat and cap and muffler and mittens and said good-bye.

When Ma shut the door behind him, she pulled in the latchstring. Then she closed and barred the wooden window shutters. It was almost dark, and Pa had not come.

Quietly, they ate supper. Then they washed the dishes and swept the hearth.

Out in the dark, the wind shrieked and howled. It rattled the door latch and shook the shutters. It screamed down the chimney, and the fire roared and flared.

All that time, Laura and Mary listened for the sound of wagon wheels. They knew Ma was listening, too, while she rocked and sang Carrie to sleep.

When Carrie fell asleep, Ma went on rocking. At last she undressed Carrie and put her to bed. Laura and Mary looked at each other. They didn't want to go to bed.

"Bedtime, girls!" said Ma.

Laura begged to be allowed to sit up until Pa came home. Mary begged, too. Finally, Ma said they could.

For a long, long time they sat up. Mary yawned, and then Laura yawned. But they kept their eyes wide open. Laura's eyes saw things grow very large and then very small. Sometimes she saw two Marys, and sometimes she couldn't see at all. But she was going to sit up until Pa came home.

Suddenly a terrible crash scared her, and Ma gently picked her up. She had fallen right off the bench, smack on the floor!

She tried to tell Ma that she wasn't sleepy, but an enormous yawn cut off her words. She let Ma tuck her under the warm covers.

But in the middle of the night, she sat straight up. Ma was sitting still in the rocking chair by the fire. Mary's eyes were open, and Jack was pacing up and down. The door latch rattled and the shutters shook. A wild howl rose and fell and rose again.

"What's that howling?" Laura asked.

"The wind is howling," said Ma. "Lie down, Laura, and go to sleep."

Laura lay back down, but her eyes would not shut. She knew Pa was out in that terrible howling.

Ma began to sway gently in the rocking chair. Laura didn't know that she had gone to sleep again. But suddenly her eyes opened, and she saw Pa standing by the fire.

She jumped out of bed, shouting, "Oh, Pa! Pa!"

Pa's boots were caked with frozen mud. His nose was red with cold, and his hair stood up wildly on his head. He was so cold that coldness came through Laura's nightgown when she reached him.

"Wait!" he said. He wrapped Laura in

68

Ma's big shawl, and then he hugged her.

Everything was all right. The house was cozy with firelight. There was the warm, brown smell of coffee. Ma was smiling, and Pa was there.

The shawl was so large that Mary wrapped the other end of it around her. Pa pulled off his stiff boots and warmed his stiff, cold hands. Then he sat on the bench. He took Mary on one knee and Laura on the other. He hugged them against him, all snuggled in the shawl. Their bare toes toasted in the heat from the fire.

"Ah!" Pa sighed. "I thought I never would get here."

Ma looked through the things Pa had brought from town. She found the brown sugar and spooned it into a tin cup.

"Your coffee will be ready in a minute, Charles," she said.

Pa told them about the trip to town and back.

"It rained the whole way there," Pa said. "And then, on the way back, the mud froze between the spokes of the wheels until they were nearly solid. I had to keep getting out to knock the mud loose, so the horses could pull the wagon."

Pa said that the terrible wind had started while he was in town. People there had told him that he better wait until it blew itself out, but he wanted to get home to his girls.

"I never saw such a wind," Pa said, shaking his head. "It cuts like a knife."

He drank his hot coffee and wiped his mustache with his handkerchief.

"Ah! That hits the spot, Caroline!" he said. "Now I'm beginning to thaw out."

Then his eyes twinkled at Ma, and he

told her to open the square package on the table.

"Be careful," he said. "Don't drop it."

"Oh, Charles!" Ma said. "You didn't!"

"Open it," Pa said.

Ma unwrapped the package. Inside there were eight small squares of glass for the windows. Now they would have glass windows in their house! Not one of the squares was broken. Pa had brought them safely all the way home.

Ma shook her head and said he shouldn't have spent so much. But her whole face was smiling, and Pa laughed with joy. Laura and Mary were happy, too. All winter long they would be able to look out the windows as much as they liked, and the warm, bright sunshine would come in.

Pa said he thought that Ma and Mary

72

and Laura would like glass windows better than any other present, and he was right. They did.

But the windows were not all he had brought. There was a little paper sack full of pure white sugar. Ma opened it, and Mary and Laura looked at the sparkling whiteness of that beautiful sugar. Ma gave them each a taste of it from a spoon. Then Ma tied it carefully up. They would have white sugar when company came.

Best of all, Pa was safely home again. Now he had nails to give back to Mr. Edwards, and cornmeal, and fat pork, and salt, and everything they needed. He would not have to go to town again for a long time.

Laura and Mary went back to sleep, very comfortable all over. Everything was all right when Pa was there.

Come Home to Little House!

THE ROSE
CHAPTER BOOK COLLECTION

Adapted from the Rose Years books
by Roger Lea MacBride
Illustrated by Doris Ettlinger

THE CAROLINE
CHAPTER BOOK COLLECTION

Adapted from the Caroline Years books
by Maria D. Wilkes
Illustrated by Doris Ettlinger